Transportation

DATE DUE

WORKING ANIMALS

Transportation

Robert Grayson

Marshall Cavendish
Benchmark
New York

This edition first published by Marshall Cavendish Benchmark in 2011
Copyright © 2011 Amber Books Ltd

Published by Marshall Cavendish Benchmark
An imprint of Marshall Cavendish Corporation

Other Marshall Cavendish Offices:
Marshall Cavendish International (Asia) Private Limited, 1 New Industrial Road, Singapore 536196 • Marshall Cavendish International (Thailand) Co Ltd. 253 Asoke, 12th Flr, Sukhumvit 21 Road, Klongtoey Nua, Wattana, Bangkok 10110, Thailand • Marshall Cavendish (Malaysia) Sdn Bhd, Times Subang, Lot 46, Subang Hi-Tech Industrial Park, Batu Tiga, 40000 Shah Alam, Selangor Darul Ehsan, Malaysia

Marshall Cavendish is a trademark of Times Publishing Limited

All websites were available and accurate when this book was sent to press.

Library of Congress Cataloging-in-Publication Data

Grayson, Robert, 1951-
   Transportation / Robert Grayson.
      p. cm.
   Includes index.
   Summary: "Describes animals that people all over the world use to transport people and goods, such as elephants, horses, yaks, water buffalo, and dogs"–Provided by publisher.
   ISBN 978-1-60870-167-4
   1. Pack animals (Transportation)–Juvenile literature. I. Title.
   HE153.G73 2010
   636.088'2–dc22
                                        2010006899

Editorial and design by
Amber Books Ltd
Bradley's Close
74–77 White Lion Street
London N1 9PF
United Kingdom
www.amberbooks.co.uk

Project Editor: James Bennett
Copy Editor: Peter Mavrikis
Design: Andrew Easton
Picture Research: Terry Forshaw, Natascha Spargo

Printed in China
135642

CONTENTS

Chapter 1
Going Places

The steadiness of llamas, the power of horses, the strength of elephants, the endurance of camels, the muscle of oxen, the teamwork of huskies, the toughness of donkeys—all these features make for outstanding workers, haulers, or pack animals.

Each of these animals has special talents. Some of them can travel long distances for many hours in the extreme heat, while others can easily handle the bitter cold. Others can climb rough, narrow trails with heavy loads on their backs. Still others can pull wagons through wetlands or timber through thick jungles.

Animals have played a major role in the history of transportation throughout the world. Long before there were motor vehicles of any kind, animals made important

◀ **Tourists on safari in India ride atop a giant Indian elephant.**

▲ **Nepal's high mountains are a test for a donkey's transportation skills.**

contributions when it came to getting people and goods from one place to another. Every part of the world has particular animals that adapt to the climate, trails, and needs of the people looking for a ride—camels in the desert, elephants in the jungle, donkeys and llamas in the mountains.

For thousands of years, our ancestors either walked or relied on animals to move from one place to another. Even though the invention of the wheel made it possible for people to develop two-wheeled carts in ancient times, there were no roads back then, so the carts could not

▼ **Farmers all over the world, like this one in Alförd, Hungary, still use horses to carry their bales of hay and bring their crops to market.**

Green Transportation

While some might say that using animals for transportation purposes is old-fashioned, those interested in saving the environment would disagree.
If elephants were not used for logging in the dense forests of Myanmar in Southeast Asia, for example, **log skidders** would be the next best choice. Moving these huge machines through the forest causes severe damage to the countryside. In addition, the fuel used to run the log skidders pollutes the air! Elephants' feet do not destroy the landscape and the huge beasts do not need gasoline to keep them running. Animals like elephants, camels, donkeys, and horses are green transportation at its best.

▲ **Elephants are patiently taught to move logs in Thailand.**

"*Even though the invention of the wheel made it possible for people to develop two-wheeled carts, there were no roads back then, so the carts could not travel very far.*"

travel very far. Animals were still the best way to take trips or carry goods.

When the Romans began building roads around 300 BCE, people figured out how to hitch horses and oxen to the two-wheeled carts. As roads were built throughout the Roman Empire, this type of animal-powered transportation became a great way for people to travel and transport goods.

▼ **Native Americans, like these Sioux Indians, photographed in the late nineteenth century, relied on horses for transportation.**

Taking the Heat

Horses played a major role in the history of firefighting, especially during the 1800s, when modern firefighting equipment, such as fire wagons with water tanks and hoses, was being invented to help pour more water onto a burning building. The equipment was heavy for firefighters to pull to the scene of a blaze, so horses were employed to handle the task.

Horses pulling these wagons saved many buildings and countless lives in cities all over the world. When the fire bell rang, a team of two or three horses living in stables in neighborhood firehouses would be hitched to the firefighting equipment before fearlessly galloping toward the fire scene. The horses gained the respect of their human co-workers and formed a strong bond with them. Many firefighting units still have plaques and monuments in their fire stations commemorating the bravery of these horses.

▲ **Before the invention of motorized fire trucks, strong, well-trained horses routinely hauled heavy equipment for fire departments all over the world.**

The four-wheeled coach was developed in eastern Europe in the 1500s. The coaches were very well made, had comfortable seats, and were completely enclosed, offering passengers protection from bad weather. These coaches, drawn by teams of well-trained horses, caught the attention of the British. They loved this new invention, and by the 1600s horse-drawn coaches were carrying people, goods, and mail all over Britain.

In the 1800s, teams of strong horses were helping pioneers settle the American West. People would pack all their belongings in a covered wagon, hitch it up to a team of

▼ **Until 1869, the only way for settlers to go west in the United States was by using a wagon pulled by horses.**

▶ **In the Peruvian Andes, the llama is the pack animal of choice. This llama is loaded with clothing for export.**

horses, and head west to start new ranches and farms.

Miners rushed to California when gold was discovered there in 1848. But they needed donkeys or mules to help carry their supplies along rugged trails. Teams of donkeys were used on these crossings, along with some horses.

Animal Transportation Today

Throughout the world, people still rely on animal power to transport goods and to travel along rocky, steep trails that are impossible for motor vehicles to climb.

In the Arctic, teams of dogs are used to pull people on sleds across icy, snow-packed trails. Animals are still the only way to get across hot, sandy deserts or push through the thick undergrowth of steamy, wet rain forests. In these remote areas, animals provide the only means of getting goods to market and necessities like water back home.

But animals are not machines. As living creatures, they must be trained to do the jobs they are being asked to do. While a camel may be able to walk long distances in the Sahara Desert without stopping for water or taking a rest, it must be tamed and trained before it can work.

A llama can carry heavy loads for miles in the Andes Mountains of South America, but it, too, must be trained, properly **conditioned**, and treated humanely in order to get the job done right. Elephants can use their trunks to move heavy logs in the forests of Thailand, but only if they are patiently taught. Even in today's modern world, animals are still keeping people and goods on the move.

▲ **Camels evolved to survive in hot, dusty deserts with little water.**

The Great Race of Mercy

Sled dogs are responsible for one of the most dramatic transportation feats in recorded history: the rescue of a remote town in northwest Alaska. In January 1925, when a deadly diphtheria epidemic threatened Nome, the town lacked the serum that was used to both prevent the disease and treat people if they did get sick. Without the serum, the town would be doomed. While there was some serum in the city of Anchorage, there was no way of getting it to the people of Nome. Airplanes at that time could not fly in the −65 degree Fahrenheit (−54 degree Celsius) temperatures that were common in that arctic region.

The only solution was to ship the medicine by train as far north as possible. That got the serum to Nenana, Alaska. The next 674 miles (1,085 kilometers) to Nome would have to be covered by dog sled. Normally, it took twenty-five days to make the trip in ideal conditions. But the serum was needed immediately.

Nineteen dog-sled teams were set up in a relay route across the frozen countryside. They traveled twenty-four hours a day through brutal cold and blizzard conditions, carrying the serum over the trail in a record five and a half days. Nearly everyone in Nome survived the epidemic. The courageous work of the dogs and the people who led them has come to be known as the Great Race of Mercy.

▲ **The famous Iditarod Trail Dog Sled Race honors the historic 1925 serum run.**

Chapter 2
Animals for Riding

Good, reliable transportation is a vital part of life, whether that transportation is in the form of a motor vehicle or a trusted, well-trained, and well-cared-for mount. Humans have ridden animals for transportation since prehistoric times.

Dashing in the Desert

Camels are still the best transportation for desert dwellers, and have been for more than 3,500 years. Camels can live on little food and water. How? In either one hump or two, depending on the breed, the animal stores fat (not water) to burn as energy during long periods when food is unavailable. Throughout its body, the camel stores water, so that it can go for a long time under dry conditions.

Camels can go for a month without fresh water, but when water is

◀ **A two-hump Bactrian camel and its rider cross the desert in western China.**

▲ **Camels stock up on water at an oasis in a desert in the Middle East.**

available, a camel can really guzzle—30 gallons (114 liters) in about twelve minutes. Some small cars can't hold 30 gallons of gas in their tanks!

The one-hump Dromedary camel thrives in the Middle East and North Africa. It lives in extreme heat most of the time. During the day, temperatures in the Sahara Desert can soar to 125 degrees Fahrenheit (52 degrees Celsius) and then plunge to below freezing at night—an adjustment the Dromedary camel easily makes.

The two-hump Bactrian camel, by contrast, is native to Mongolia and

▼ **Bedouin men ride Dromedary camels in the hot Egyptian desert.**

An Unusual Ride

How do people know which animals made good **mounts**? They take a test ride. Through the years people believed that particular animals would make for good rides from place to place, but sometimes they didn't. For example, many people thought that because zebras so closely resembled horses, the zebra would be a natural for riding or pulling carts.

   Not so. Zebras proved to be unpredictable, lacked endurance, and panicked easily. But there is always the exception. In 1907 Dr. Rosendo Ribeiro traveled the countryside of Nairobi, Kenya, making house calls on his fully trained zebra. It was quite a strange sight, even in Africa.

▲ **In rare instances, people have been able to train zebras to do the work of horses. In 1930 this zebra in Calcutta, India, was used to pull a wagonload of people. Usually, however, zebras want no part of a horse's duties.**

China, places of extreme cold. In the region's harsh Gobi Desert, winter temperatures can fall to –60 degrees Fahrenheit (–51degrees Celsius). The Bactrian camel has a heavy coat to deal with the frigid temperatures. It sheds its coat when warmer weather arrives.

For reliability in the desert, nothing tops a camel, which can close its nostrils to keep out grit. Two rows of lengthy and heavy eyelashes provide great eye protection. And a camel will not sink into the sand dunes. With its two-toed foot, connected by a web of skin, it successfully makes its way in the continuously shifting sand.

A camel weighs between 1,000 and 1,450 pounds (454–658 kilograms) and stands anywhere

▼ **The camel is a great desert traveler because the skin between its toes spreads out and keeps the camel from sinking into the desert sands.**

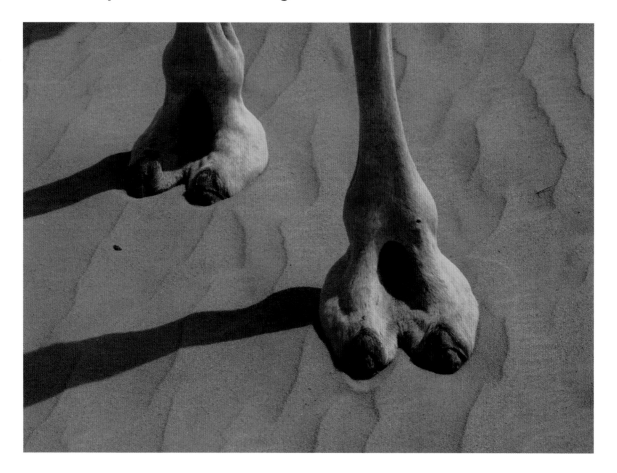

▲ **An elephant is employed as a taxi in Jaipur, India.**

from 6 to 7.5 feet (1.8–2.3 meters) tall. A big, husky camel moves at about 5 miles (8 kilometers) an hour and can go 50 miles (80 kilometers) or so in a day. A smaller camel moves faster and goes farther, so many frequent desert travelers seek out the smaller variety. If the rider doesn't tire, neither will the camel, which can go nonstop for eighteen straight hours.

Heavy-Duty Ride

One of the most powerful rides in the world is an elephant. Even the smaller Asian elephant weighs between 6,000 and 11,000 pounds (2,700–5,000 kilograms) and stands 7 to 11.5 feet (2–3.5 meters) tall. The massive African elephant weighs between 8,000 and 15,000 pounds (3,600–6,800 kilograms) and grows from 9 to 13 feet (3–4 meters) tall.

❝From atop an elephant, police can see anybody trying to hide from them, even in thick jungle foliage.❞

Both elephants are named for the continent where they live, but the Asian elephant is the calmer of the two and therefore used more often for riding.

In rural Laos and Vietnam, in Southeast Asia, elephants are one of the few means of transportation for villagers living in remote areas. In India, law enforcement officers ride elephants in the jungle, tracking down people who illegally hunt and kill elephants and other protected species. From atop an elephant, police can see anybody trying to hide from them, even in thick jungle foliage. People in southern India dress elephants in stunning outfits and ride them as part of religious ceremonies. In the city of Bangkok, Thailand, elephants are used as taxis to carry tourists to and from local events and hotels. In zoos all over the world, elephants give visitors an **aerial** view by providing rides throughout the zoo grounds. The ever-steady elephant can walk about 4 miles (6.5 kilometers) an hour and run for short distances, reaching a speed of 25 miles (40 kilometers) per hour.

Horsepower

What is the preferred ride of cattle ranchers in the United States and Australia? The horse, of course! Only horses can herd cattle, which often graze in areas a car could never reach. Ranchers can sit tall in the saddle, observing everything that's happening with the herd.

Equines have long earned their place as reliable and loyal transportation. People who work with horses every day develop a special relationship with them.

▶ **Tracking tigers, as this man is doing in the Kanha National Park in India, is much easier and safer atop an elephant.**

Horse and rider trust each other and work as a trained team. Police, for example, use horses to keep law and order. Horses leave cars in the dust when it comes to crowd control, patrolling parks, or conducting searches in mountainous areas.

There are more than 350 breeds of horses and ponies, but the most popular for riding are the quarter horse, named for its ability to beat any other type of horse in a quarter-mile race, and the Morgan horse. When fully grown, either of these American horse breeds can weigh well over 1,300 pounds (600 kilograms).

Mules and donkeys—both part of the horse family—are used to transport people along uneven and rocky trails. While they're frequently used in developing countries, they're also a common sight in Arizona's Grand Canyon, where they carry tourists down the treacherous slopes.

◄ **A young boy on horseback herds sheep and goats in Mongolia, a huge country where there are few roads.**

▲ **Cowboys all over the world are famous for their riding skills and their love of horses.**

Peak Performer

Though rarely seen in the West, yaks are prized in mountainous regions around the world. Exceptionally surefooted, Yaks have no problem traveling along dangerous, narrow slopes. Their soft coat of fur forms a cushion for the rider and keeps the animal warm in the cold mountains. **Domesticated** yaks weigh between 500 and 1,300 pounds (230–600 kilograms). Yaks are at their best on high mountain peaks because they can breathe easily when oxygen is in low supply. Most animals don't have big enough lungs to breathe at an altitude of 20,000 feet (6,100 meters) or higher. But yaks are right at home in places like the vast, mountainous Himalayan region of Asia, where peaks exceed 23,000 feet (7,000 meters).

◀ **The sure-footed yak's heavy coat keeps him warm at high altitudes.**

▲ **In Tibet a man rides one of his yaks while others carry his belongings.**

❝Ostriches, which have big, bulky bodies and strong, powerful legs, do not mind carrying a person. ❞

Big Bird

It is a mode of transportation that not many people think of, but riding an ostrich is not uncommon in some places of the world. They do it easily in South Africa.

Ostriches are the largest birds in the world, reaching 8 feet (2.4 meters) tall and weighing close to 250 pounds (113 kilograms). They can move as fast as 40 miles (64 kilometers) an hour without a rider and 35 miles (56 kilometers) an hour with a rider. These extraordinary-looking birds have big, bulky bodies and strong, powerful legs, and they don't mind carrying a person.

In South Africa, where there are many ostrich farms, workers can be seen riding ostriches like horses as they travel from one part of the farm to another.

▲ **These ostrich farm workers are racing on a specially constructed track.**

Ancient Wild Ride

It has been reported that the Egyptian Queen Arsinoe, who lived over two thousand years ago, had her own ostrich and would use a saddle to ride the big bird on a regular basis. During roughly the same period, ancient Egyptians were able to train the impressive-looking birds to pull carts. In the late 1800s and early 1900s, ostriches drew carts loaded with children as an amusement ride in zoos in Europe and the United States. People still ride ostriches to this day.

▲ **It takes a lot of skill to master the art of balancing oneself on the back of an ostrich. Once achieved, however, it can be quite a ride!**

Chapter 3
Pack Animals

For thousands of years, people have loaded the goods they made or grew on the back of a sturdy pack animal to begin the long journey to the marketplace to sell their products.

In South America, the best pack animal is a llama. Intelligent and easy to train, llamas weigh between 250 and 450 pounds (114–204 kilograms) and stand as tall as 6 feet (1.8 meters). They can carry between 80 and 100 pounds (36–45 kilograms) for 15 miles (24 kilometers) a day, navigating steep, rocky trails at high altitudes in the Andes Mountains.

Llamas, which are members of the camel family, can live on little or poor-quality food for long periods of

◀ **Experienced llamas help a camper in Idaho carry some of his gear.**

▲ **Llamas are friendly, calm, and dependable animals.**

time. They don't mind eating the few varieties of plants that grow on the mountainside. These mountain dwellers have a lush coat of fur that protects them from the cold.

The Incas, an Indian people who once ruled a vast area along the western coast of South America, first domesticated llamas thousands of years ago. They were impressed by how calm, friendly, and gentle these animals were. In the hills of Peru and Chile today, when a llama is packed up with a villager's belongings for a trip, a child often sits on the llama, too. There is no danger of the child

▼ **Llamas work best when they are well packed. The llama's load needs to be spread out evenly on its body.**

Silent Brothers

Very few civilizations value their beasts of burden. In fact, most seem to take them for granted. But that was not the case with the Incas, who worshiped the llama, their reliable animal companion.

The Inca Empire (1200 to 1533) was an advanced civilization located in present-day Peru, in South America. The Incas built beautiful temples, constructed a network of roads, and developed vast irrigation systems. For all these things they needed llamas to help carry building materials to worksites. Some of these sites would have been extremely difficult, if not impossible, to reach with the necessary materials if it had not been for the hardworking llama.

As long as they were well cared for, the llamas would continue to work no matter how difficult the terrain. In cold weather Inca workers could even lie down next to their furry animal co-workers for a bit of warmth.

The Incas so revered their beasts of burden that they referred to them as their "silent brothers."

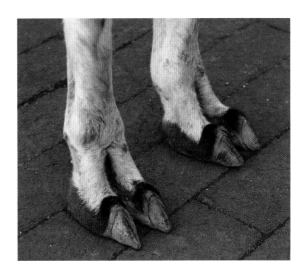

▲ **A llama's foot is padded on the bottom and has two toes.**

falling off the llama because this pack animal is extremely sure-footed, even in the steepest terrain. Alert at all times, llamas see trouble—like a soft spot near the edge of a trail—and sidestep it.

If a llama's load is too heavy, the animal will lie down and refuse to move. Just like a camel, it might also show its displeasure by spitting. Llamas will act the same way if a load is loosely packed and keeps shifting or is not balanced properly on its back.

It could take a year to train a llama to be a pack animal. But training isn't wasted on these superb mountain climbers because they never forget their skills. If they are treated well, they remain fiercely loyal.

These rock climbers are not the only ones who have to be trained, however. People need to learn how to pack a llama properly before a trip. Natives of the Andes Mountains pass this knowledge down through the generations.

Over the Long Haul

Packing skills are needed when loading a mule or a donkey as well. Mules and donkeys are very calm, playful, and friendly animals and don't get frightened by loud or startling noises along the trail, as horses often do.

A mule—the product of a male donkey and female horse—is usually

▼ Donkeys are calm and dependable pack animals. These donkeys are transporting supplies along a steep path near the Grand Canyon.

Not So Stubborn

When most people think of donkeys or mules, the first thing that comes to mind is that they are stubborn. But that is really not true. Mules and donkeys are very smart and learn things quickly. They won't move if they are not packed properly. They won't go anywhere they think is against their self-interest. So, if they believe that a trail is unsafe, they will simply stop walking and refuse to move—hence the term "stubborn as a mule." But they are not being **ornery**; they are simply being cautious.

▲ **Donkeys stop to nibble as they carry water along a mountain trail on an island off the west coast of Africa.**

« Donkeys and mules, which can withstand extreme heat, are found throughout Central and South America. »

much bigger than a donkey. Some mules can grow to be as big as a horse—upwards of 1,000 pounds (454 kilograms). So mules can carry heavier loads than donkeys, and they are stronger than most horses. Mules also have better endurance than horses—they can carry loads longer and farther. Depending on the size of the mule, the animal can carry between 150 and 300 pounds (68–136 kilograms) over 15 to 20 miles (24–32 kilometers) in a ten-hour period. A donkey will carry a

▲ **A donkey displays goods for sale on a street in Mexico.**

▶ **This heavily packed cart seems way too big for the mule that is going to pull it.**

slightly lighter load, because it's smaller, but it can keep moving for about the same amount of time. Both donkeys and mules can work as pack animals into their old age.

Donkeys and mules, which can withstand extreme heat, are found throughout Central and South America, carrying everything from supplies like flour and seeds to grains that have been harvested. They are also used as pack animals in other parts of the world, such as Africa and Asia, because they are more economical than horses. Donkeys and mules eat less and work harder than horses. And, while horses do best on level trails, donkeys and mules can navigate rough and hilly terrain.

Himalayan Hauler

Yaks are great pack animals for the same reasons that they are highly sought-after rides: They are strong, steady, and reliable at high altitudes. No other animal could do the job yaks do in the Himalayas, especially

Pack Goats

Hikers in the midwestern United States are finding that it is much more enjoyable to hike trails with a friendly goat carrying their gear. Goats are sure-footed, and eat brush and weeds along the trail so hikers do not have to bring any costly special food along for their animal hiking companion.

Goats can weigh as much as 200 pounds (91 kilograms) and can carry between 50 and 70 pounds (23–32 kilograms) for roughly 10 miles (16 kilometers) without rest. If need be, goats can actually go for three days without water.

Goats adapt well to carrying pack loads with very little training, and they are not prone to acting jittery on the trail. Goats do not need to wear a leash while hiking. They follow alongside humans, much as dogs do, and will not run off. Goats can be left loose in camp when hikers go to sleep for the night.

▶ **One of the places where yaks are most commonly used is in the Himalayas, the mountain range that includes Mount Everest.**

❝No other animal could do the job yaks do in the Himalayas, especially when it comes to carrying heavy loads over treacherous, winding trails.❞

when it comes to carrying heavy loads over treacherous, winding trails—trails too tough for other animals to manage.

Blessed with excellent hearing, yaks can pick up unusual or dangerous sounds, like falling rock, far enough in advance to avoid walking into trouble. This big member of the ox family is easy to train for pack-carrying missions, and its small split hoof lets it step

▲ Camels are employed regularly for transport in the Tunisian desert.

loaded yak with a tight pack can cover 3.5 miles (5.5 kilometers) an hour in the mountains.

Ship of the Desert

Another animal that travels in caravans is the camel. Known as the "ship of the desert," camels can carry loads of 450 pounds (204 kilograms), but have been known to hold as much as 900 pounds (400 kilograms). A loaded camel can walk about 2 miles (3 kilometers) in an hour, and caravans of packed camels are known to cover between 12 and 15 miles (19–24 kilometers) in a day.

To make trips across the desert easier for both camels and their human companions, most desert travelers like to start out at dusk or during the night, when the sand is cooler and the sun is not beating down. Camels usually prefer to walk, rather than move at a faster pace, especially if the sand is hot. But they can gallop or trot while carrying a heavy load, if required.

effortlessly along the rough trail, avoiding foot injuries.

Large yaks can carry up to 150 pounds (68 kilograms), and these animals don't mind traveling in **caravans** to share the load. A fully

▶ Caravans of dromedary camels such as this can often be seen traveling along the dunes of the Sahara Desert at sunset, when the temperature drops.

Chapter 4
Pulling Vehicles

Pure, brute strength is what it takes for an animal to pull carts and wagons loaded with people, tree trunks, and even rocks. These draft animals labor on dirt roads, along muddy paths, in thick jungles, and sometimes on snow-covered trails.

Buffalo Power

Among the most powerful **draft animals** are water buffalo, found in great numbers all over Asia. Some are used in farming, but many pull carts loaded with much-needed firewood. Growing to 6 feet (1.8 meters) long and weighing between 1,500 and 2,700 pounds (680–1,225 kilograms), these slow but powerful mammals can pull upwards of 1,600 pounds (725 kilograms). What makes water buffalo especially valuable in countries like Vietnam and Cambodia is that, as

◄ **Hardworking oxen pull a cart in Myanmar.**

▲ **A water buffalo drags a heavy log in the forests of northern Vietnam.**

their name implies, they do not mind standing in or moving through water.

Many animals steer clear of wetlands, but the husky water buffalo wade right through them, and they are not slowed down by mud, either. They have wide-**splayed** hooves that keep them from sinking into the muddy trails in Asian rain forests and allow them to travel through water as if they were walking on land. Water buffalo have one drawback, however: They only like to work five hours a day, and when they are tired they will sit down on the job and not move again until they are ready.

▼ **Water buffalo are excellent swimmers and do not mind carrying a person across deep rivers, like this one in the Mekong Delta in Vietnam.**

Elephant School

In Thailand and Myanmar, Asian elephants are key players in the logging industry. With their long trunks, they are trained to do heavy lifting and pushing. They learn to move logs out of a forest and place them in a nearby river. From there the river carries the logs downstream to a timber yard, where they will be processed.

In Myanmar, the logging season lasts for eight months out of the year. The elephants work so hard during that time that they can lose close to 1,000 pounds (454 kilograms) each.

▲ **This hardworking elephant carries a teak log through a forest in Thailand.**

Super Strong

Another powerful **tow animal** is the ox. Depending on the breed, an ox can weigh anywhere from 500 to 3,000 pounds (225–1,350 kilograms). Oxen work well in pairs, especially for hauling, and can pull a substantial amount of weight. They are stronger and work harder than most horses. Oxen do not give up in the face of a challenge. If prompted, they will continue to try to drag the heaviest of loads. They are relatively easy to train, too, more so than other draft animals. An ox learns quickly and usually doesn't forget.

Different breeds of oxen have adapted to various regions of the world. Many are used in teams to pull carts or wagons loaded with

▼ **In Madagascar, oxen can often be seen pulling carts. Here they transport sacks of charcoal for sale at the local market.**

《《 *Oxen work well in pairs, especially for hauling, and can pull a substantial amount of weight.* **》》**

heavy goods. They move equally well on dry land and through wetlands and are very dependable. Once trained, oxen rarely run off.

No Horsing Around

Strong, muscular horses have been specially bred for heavy pulling work. Some, like the Percheron, found in northern France, weigh more than 2,000 pounds (900 kilograms) and have little body fat. Rugged and powerful, these horses are trained to do heavy work. Shire horses, which are native to England, weigh about 1,600 pounds (725

Dogs for Pulling, Dogs for Packing

While not considered pack animals, large dogs were sometimes used for that purpose by Native Americans back in the sixteenth and seventeenth centuries. The dogs were able to carry loads weighing from 60 to 70 pounds (27–32 kilograms). Often there was no other means of transportation available except a dog. For example, if a family's horses were used to transport the children or the elderly, the only "pack" animal left was the dog. If the family members were lucky, they had more than one dog.

The dogs performed well as pack animals. They could even be taught to bark or howl when an item in their packs came loose or fell off. Once taught to carry a pack, the dogs would remember how to perform the task even if months or years passed before they had to do it again.

Native Americans also used large dogs as draft animals. They pulled small wagons carrying supplies or sick or injured people. Dogs most commonly used in these roles were mixed breeds—including part wolf—and highly intelligent. They usually joined humans voluntarily, often entering Native American camps on their own.

❝The word horsepower is still used to describe engine power, referring to how many horses it would take to produce the same power a motor is putting out.❞

kilograms) and are often used to cart tree trunks out of a forest when tractors can't get near the load. Shires will work as a team if a load is too heavy for one horse.

These muscular horses will pull everything from wagons full of hay to coaches full of people. As a **testament** to the strength of horses, the word *horsepower* is still used to describe engine power, referring to how many horses it would take to produce the same power a motor is putting out.

▲ **Suffolk Punch horses handle heavy forestry work in England.**

▶ **The Budweiser Clydesdales are the most famous draft team in the world.**

“More than seventy French towns have started using horse-drawn carts to do everything from taking children to school to collecting garbage.”

In 2007 the government of France decided to help curb global warming by asking people to use horses instead of motor vehicles whenever possible. More than seventy French towns have started using horse-drawn carts to do everything from taking children to school to collecting garbage and helping with street cleaning. Around the world, many cities now offer visitors sightseeing tours in horse-drawn carriages.

Some people, like the Amish in Pennsylvania, still rely on horse-drawn carriages for transportation. In parts of eastern Europe, too, horses still help farmers get their crops to market.

▲ Even to this day, Amish farmers transport hay by means of a horse and cart. Horses play an important role in transportation for the Amish.

Kind of a Drag

Until the 1900s, many Native Americans traveled over land that lent itself better to dragging something than pulling it in a cart with wheels. Plains tribes of North America used a flat, wooden device called a travois, attached to a horse, to drag their belongings from place to place. The triangle-shaped travois was one of the more effective wheelless transports of its time. The simple construction consisted of a platform attached to two long poles. A cloth could be stretched over the frame to help hold goods in place, though once packed, the goods still had to be tied down.

The travois allowed a horse to drag more weight than it could carry on its back. The travois worked well because the Native Americans mostly moved through areas of soft soil and forest land, and at times over land covered by snow. A cart's wheels would have sunk into the earth and forced the horse to strain to pull the cart out of one rut after another.

▲ **Native Americans used a travois, which has no wheels and is pulled by a horse, as an effective means of transportation.**

❝Even though it might be their nature to go their own way, these spirited dogs must learn to work in teams of six to ten and follow the lead dog.❞

Not Your Average Dog's Life

Wagons and carts will not get the job done in the Arctic cold, so people who have to get around in the frozen North use sleds pulled by teams of carefully bred and well-trained dogs. Siberian Huskies are just one of the breeds that work in these bitter-cold regions, where temperatures can drop to –40 degrees Fahrenheit (–40 degrees Celsius).

Alaskan Malamutes and Samoyeds are among the other breeds. These winter travelers are strong, tough, muscular dogs that weigh between 60 and 85 pounds (27–39 kilograms). They are loyal, friendly, and smart. Many people who work with them believe they remember trails after having been on them just once.

Even though it might be their nature to go their own way, these spirited dogs must learn to work in teams of six to ten and follow the lead dog. Only the most experienced trainers can produce the **caliber** of dog that can mean the difference between life and death on a frozen, barren trail.

▶ **A good dogsled team is crucial in the Arctic cold.**

The Real Rudolph

In the cold regions of Siberia and Scandinavia, reindeer are used to pull sleds across the snow and ice. Small sleds can be pulled by one reindeer, but bigger sleds need a team.

Reindeer have big hooves, which give them a good grip on the ice.

A reindeer weighs in at about 300 pounds (136 kilograms). It has a thick coat of fur, which protects it against winter winds. Reindeer need to be well trained to learn how to pull a sled. But once they learn this skill, these northern beasts can pull twice their weight for 40 miles (64 kilometers) a day.

▲ **Teams of reindeer haul people and goods over vast distances in the frigid cold of western Siberia.**

Chapter 5
Career Guide

With so many animals being used for riding, hauling, and pulling around the world, it's important that they are well cared for and treated humanely.

Unfortunately, many countries do not police the treatment of animals, but there are numerous organizations that do. Among these are animal rights and animal welfare groups, plus international wildlife and animal conservation organizations. Employees of these groups work with animal owners worldwide to teach them how to train and care for their working animals. If you are interested in animals, one day you may want to pursue a career in animal protection.

◄ **Nature photographer Gerry Ellis is perched atop an elephant in Nepal.**

▲ **An animal welfare worker visits a sanctuary for rescued donkeys.**

Animal Welfare

A career in animal welfare gives a person a chance to make a real difference in how animals are treated. Animal welfare workers see that working animals get the medical attention they need, are given the proper amount of water, have enough to eat, are not overworked, and have the proper living quarters. Animal welfare professionals travel around the world, saving the lives of all types of animals. To pursue this field, a person needs a college background in biology

▼ **A veterinarian checks a dog's paw during a sled dog race in Alaska.**

« Admissions officers at college veterinary tech programs look for students who excel in high school science and math. »

or zoology, as well as conservation or environmental science.

Animal CSI

Forensic scientists at the Clark R. Bavin U.S. Fish and Wildlife Service Forensic Laboratory investigate crimes against wildlife, including animal abuse. Similar to CSI (crime scene investigation) cases, these scientists work to identify and catch people who commit crimes against animals in the United States and other parts of the world.

Without the dedication of these specially trained investigators, many crimes would go unsolved and the abuse would continue. Crimes against animals include the killing of endangered species and acts of cruelty that contribute to the injury or death of animals. This growing field requires a college degree in forensic science as well as some experience in conducting investigations.

Field Doctor

Veterinarians, who must attend both college and veterinary school, are in high demand in rural areas throughout the world. Developing countries, in particular, need these animal doctors to provide vaccinations and treatment for creatures that would otherwise get very little medical attention. The veterinarians also show people how to care for their working animals and check for signs of abuse. They teach them how to perform simple tasks, such as examining an animal's feet to make sure there are no embedded rocks, branches, or other material that could cause discomfort and lead to infection.

A veterinarian working with animals in far-off places in the world usually needs the help of a well-trained veterinary technician. The technician can save the doctor valuable time by doing, among other things, preliminary work on the various

Team Trainer

Not everyone who needs oxen to pull heavy loads has the luxury of putting together a finely trained team of these animals. But assembling a great team works better for both the animals and their human handlers.

Building a solid team of oxen starts with the person choosing and training the draft animals. Experienced teamsters—the people who work with the oxen—know that the animals have to be strong, not just big. Teamsters look for physical traits like a muscular neck, back, chest, and legs, and they give these beasts a brief workout before choosing them for a team.

Oxen are usually partnered in teams of two and must work well together, sharing the labor and pulling in the same direction, or the team fails. In pairing the animals, oxen that move at the same speed must be put together. Speed is not necessarily determined by the weight or size of the ox. A big ox and a slightly smaller one can move at the same speed; it comes down to **agility**. Once teamed up, the oxen are taught how to carry out the job they are given, such as hauling logs out of forests. It takes many hours to train the animals to respond to verbal commands. But the work is well worth the effort, as these teams of oxen often work together for ten years or more.

▲ **Two oxen pull a cart along a road in Lesotho in southern Africa.**

cases. Admissions officers at college veterinary tech programs look for students who excel in high school science and math and who have done volunteer work in a local veterinarian's office.

Breaking News

Wildlife photojournalists report—in words and photographs—how working animals are being treated throughout the world. This reporting can be a powerful tool in protecting animals from abuse. Photojournalists, with their stories and images, can provide clear proof of the conditions they witness. Strong written communication skills are essential for this job, as well as knowing how to take pictures that tell a story.

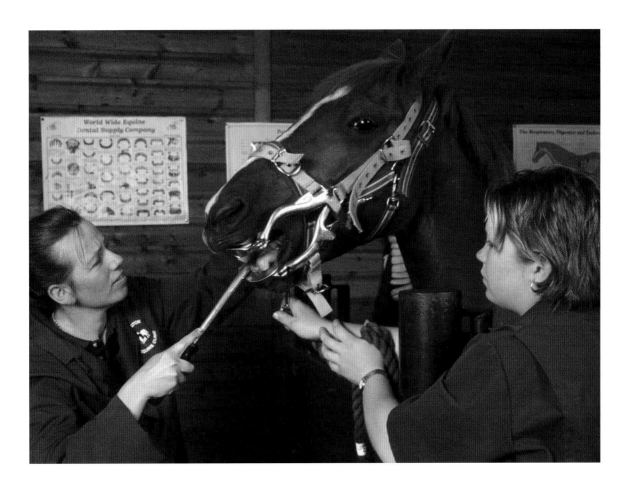

▲ **An equestrian veterinarian and her assistant examine a horse's teeth.**

Glossary

aerial
a view from above, as from high in the air

agility
the ability to move smoothly, easily, and quickly

caliber
degree of excellence; quality

caravans
groups of people who travel together

conditioned
made used to something; accustomed

domesticated
tamed or specially bred for use by humans

draft animals
animals used for pulling loads

equines
horses

forensic
relating to the use of science in the investigation of criminal cases

log skidders
motorized, gas-powered vehicles that transport logs

mounts
animals that people ride

ornery
ill-tempered

splayed
spread apart

testament
proof of something's worth

tow animal
an animal that pulls a load

Further Information

BOOKS

Arnold, Caroline. *Llama*. New York: Morrow Junior Books, 1988

Neme, Laurel A. *Animal Investigators: How the World's First Wildlife Forensics Lab Is Solving Crimes and Saving Endangered Species*. New York: Simon & Schuster, 2009.

Smith, Roland & Michael J. Schmidt. *In the Forest with the Elephants*. New York: Gulliver Green Books/Harcourt Brace & Company, 1998.

WEBSITES

http://www.nwf.org
Official site of the National Wildlife Federation

http://www.nature.org
Official site of the Nature Conservancy

http://www.worldwildlife.org
Official site of the World Wildlife Fund

www.scla.us/llamafacts.html
Official site of the South Central Llama Association

http://www.lovelongears.com
Site of the American Donkey and Mule Society

http://www.tfaoi.com/newsmu/nmus86x.htm
Official site of the International Museum of the Horse

http://nrccamel.com
National Research Center on Camel

Index

PICTURE CREDITS
The photographs in this book are used by permission and through the courtesy of:

Corbis: 2 (Layne Kennedy), 11 (Bettmann), 12 (Bettmann), 13 (Michael S. Yamashita), 16 (Wolfgang Kaehler), 27 (Craig Lovell), 28 (Patrick Robert/Sygma), 30 (Scott T. Smith), 32 (Scott T. Smith), 42 (Nik Wheeler), 44 (Paul Almasy), 45 (Michael S. Yamashita), 49 (Kevin R. Morris)

Dreamstime: 7 (Johan Karlsson), 35 (Frank Bach), 36 (Wendy Nero), 39 (Irina Efremova), 52 (Ventura69), 58 (Pg-images)

FLPA: 6 (Elliott Neep), 9 (Neil Bowman), 23 (Theo Allofs/Minden Pictures), 43 (Keith Rushforth), 46 (Frans Lanting), 48 (John Watkins), 54 (Gerry Ellis/Minden Pictures), 56 (Stefan Wackerhagen/Imagebroker), 59 (Angela Hampton)

Fotolia: 17 (Paul Prescott), 26 (Andre), 40 (Paty), 41 (Galyna Andrushko)

Getty Images: 191 (IMAGNO/Austrian Archives (S), 29 (Frans Lemmens), 34 (fStop)

iStockphoto: 14 (Alexander Hafemann), 20 (Charles Gibson), 24 (Robert Churchill/travelphotographer), 33 (Laurie Knight)

Library of Congress: 10, 51

Photos.com: 25, 31, 50

Photoshot: 8 (World Illustrated), 18 (BSIP), 21 (JTB), 53 (NHPA)

Rex Features: 55 (John Dee)

Stock Xchang: 37 (Albert Wildgen)

U.S. Department of Defense: 15

ABOUT THE AUTHOR
Robert Grayson is an award-winning former daily newspaper reporter and magazine writer. He is the author of a number of books for young adults about environmental activism and law enforcement. His published work includes stories about working animals both on stage and in the movies. These have appeared in *Cat World, Animal Companion*, and numerous other animal-related publications. An avid cat lover, Robert's essays have appeared in the anthology *Pets Across America: Lessons Animals Teach Us.*